THIS BLOOMSBURY BOOK

BELONGS TO

....

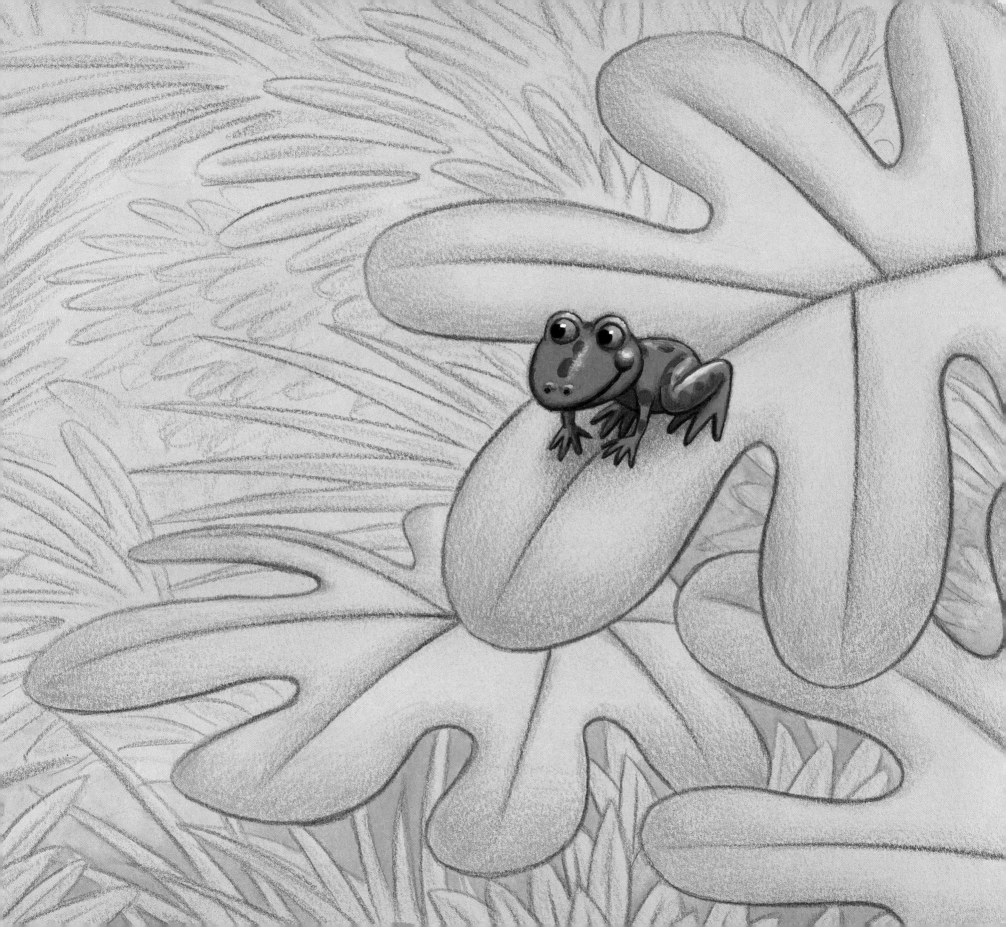

For Tessa, Glynis, Janet, Linda, Madalena and Patricia, with love – SR

To Annika and Maja – MT

First published in Great Britain in 2003 by Bloomsbury Publishing Plc
36 Soho Square, London, W1D 3QY
This paperback edition first published in 2004

Text copyright © Shen Roddie 2003
Illustrations copyright © Michael Terry 2003
The moral rights of the author and illustrator have been asserted

A CIP catalogue record of this book is available from the British Library
ISBN 978 0 7475 6489 8

Printed and bound in China by South China Printing Co

5 7 9 10 8 6 4

All papers used by Bloomsbury Publishing are natural, recyclable products made
from wood grown in well-managed forests. The manufacturing processes conform
to the environmental regulations of the country of origin.

THE GOSSIPY PARROT

by Shen Roddie

illustrations by Michael Terry

BLOOMSBURY
CHILDREN'S
BOOKS

Godfrey the parrot loved a good gossip!
He especially liked passing on rude remarks
and causing trouble . . .

'Snake says pigs have jelly bellies!'
screeched Godfrey to Pig.

'Does he?' squealed Pig, sharpening his trotters.
'I'll teach him a lesson!'

Pig wrestled with Snake.

Godfrey cheered! It gave him such a flutter!

Lion watched. *I'll teach that bird a lesson!*
he thought.

Lion grumbled, 'A trouble-maker has moved in.
He says monkeys pick fleas for tea!'

Godfrey was off!

'A trouble-maker has moved in! He says monkeys pick fleas for tea!' repeated Godfrey to Monkey.

'He says that, does he?' cried Monkey.
'I'll teach him a lesson!'

Monkey grabbed a nut.

Then Lion muttered,
'The trouble-maker says
elephants have hoses for noses!
Ha! Ha! Ha!'

Godfrey was off!

'The trouble-maker says elephants have hoses for noses! Ha! Ha! Ha!' screeched Godfrey to Elephant.

  'He does, does he? I'll teach him a lesson!' trumpeted Elephant, sucking up oceans of water.

Then Lion whispered
to Godfrey, 'The trouble-
maker says Crocodile wears
false teeth, clickety-clack!'

Godfrey was off!

'The trouble-maker says Crocodile wears false teeth, clickety-clack!' repeated Godfrey to Crocodile.

'He says that, does he? I'll teach him a lesson!' snapped Crocodile.

Then Lion said to Godfrey, 'The trouble-maker says Bee has stung his own bottom!'

Godfrey was off!

'The trouble-maker says Bee has stung his own bottom!' Godfrey told Bee.

'He says that, does he? I'll teach him a lesson!' buzzed Bee.

Then all the animals cried out, 'WHO *IS* THIS
TROUBLE-MAKER? WHERE IS HE?'

Godfrey flew off to ask Lion.
Lion snarled, 'The trouble-maker is a feathered fool!
He is right in front of you!'

Godfrey flew back to spread the news . . .

'The trouble-maker is a feathered fool!
He is right in front of you!' shrieked
Godfrey excitedly.
　'So he is!' cried Pig and Snake and
Monkey and Elephant and Crocodile
and Bee.

'Godfrey, you trouble-maker! You can't be our friend any more,' said Monkey.

'But that's so mean!' cried Godfrey.

'And so is tittle-tattle! No more gossip now, eh, Godfrey?' laughed Lion.

'No more gossip,' promised Godfrey . . .

'. . . even when Ratty says you are a noodle-head!'

And Godfrey was off before the animals could catch him!

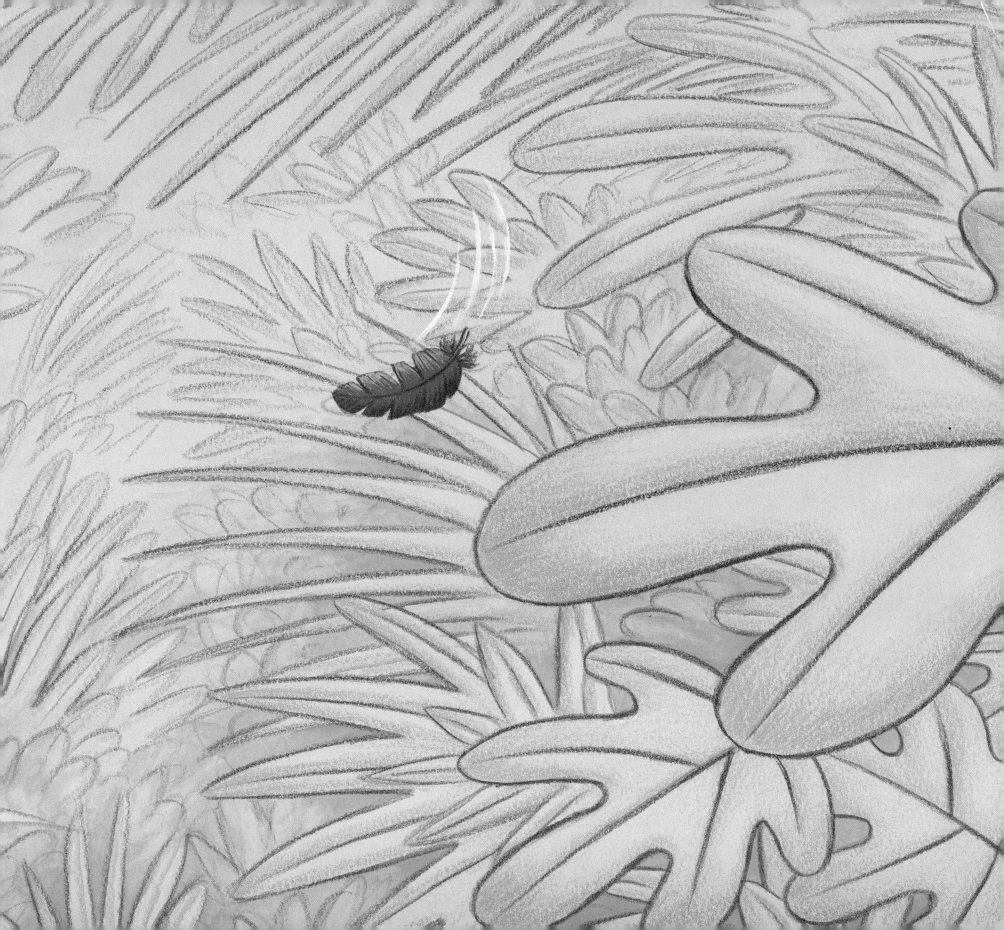

Enjoy more fabulous picture books from Shen Roddie and Michael Terry …

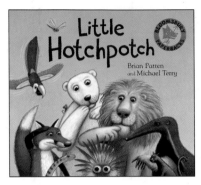

Little Hotchpotch
Brian Patten & Michael Terry

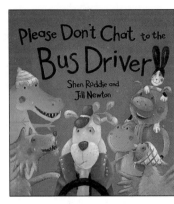

Please Don't Chat to the Bus Driver
Shen Roddie & Jill Newton

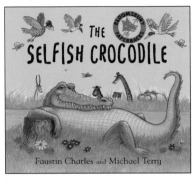

The Selfish Crocodile
Faustin Charles & Michael Terry

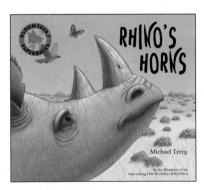

Rhino's Horns
Michael Terry

Sandbear
Shen Roddie & Jenny Jones

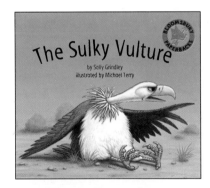

The Sulky Vulture
Sally Grindley & Michael Terry